Anna Bartlett Warner

The Shoes of Peace

Anna Bartlett Warner

The Shoes of Peace

ISBN/EAN: 9783337222475

Printed in Europe, USA, Canada, Australia, Japan

Cover: Foto ©Andreas Hilbeck / pixelio.de

More available books at **www.hansebooks.com**

THE SHOES OF PEACE.

THE

SHOES OF PEACE.

BY

ANNA B. WARNER,

AUTHOR OF "THE MELODY OF THE TWENTY-THIRD PSALM."

Ohne Hast, ohne Rast.

How beautiful are thy feet with shoes, O prince's daughter!
Canticles.

NEW YORK:

ROBERT CARTER AND BROTHERS,

530 BROADWAY.

University Press:

JOHN WILSON AND SON, CAMBRIDGE.

INTRODUCTION.

I PLEAD for a neglected bit of the Christian armour. The strong helmet, the sharp sword, the ready shield,—even the shining breast-plate,—have many wearers. But the quiet shoes are out of date. I think people well-nigh forget that such things are possible. Yet there stands the injunction :

"Your feet shod with the preparation of the gospel of peace" (Eph. vi. 15).

While the old and never-revoked promise covers all the roughness, of every road.

"Thy shoes shall be iron and brass; and as thy days, so shall thy strength be" (Deut. xxxiii. 25).

AUGUST, 1884.

CONTENTS.

———◆———

THE SHOES OF PEACE.

A CLOUD IN THE WEST.

LISTENING the other day to the rattling echoes among our hills, as gun after gun gave forth its welcome to the Twenty-second of February, I began to wonder with myself what the Father of his Country would say to this great child of his, decked in all her Nineteenth century progress? How would these almost forty States compare with the old thirteen, to those sagacious and far-seeing eyes?

It is hard, I suppose, for the wisest man
to judge fairly between his own age and
another, or even between one part and another of his own.　That early time

　"When feelings were young, and the world was new,"

must of necessity stand always apart, and
in some sort unapproachable.　Then eyes
were ignorant, and hearts untried, and
storms made no impression ; but now come
"the evil days" spoken of by the Preacher,
and "the clouds return after the rain."
Can that small, pale moon overhead, thread-
ing her way among obscuring vapours, be
possibly the very same great golden ball
that rolled up so grandly from the eastern
horizon ?　In the look of all earthly affairs
the passage of time, the growth of knowledge, must make a change.　Yet a few
things remain, for they are promised ; and
a few are unalterable, being "established

for ever." "Though a sinner do evil an hundred times, and his days be prolonged, yet surely I know that it shall be well with them that fear God, which fear before him" (Eccl. viii. 12).

With Bible help, then, it is well worth our while — it is our bounden duty — to study the age we live in. Not for its money-making facilities alone; but for its dangers, its mistakes, its drift. We all study the day's temperature, we all peer earnestly into to-morrow's weather; but the electric and magnetic conditions of the *times* are passed by unnoticed. And the few who pause to examine and dare to proclaim, are classed by the rest with those proverbial people who always carry umbrellas. "Ye can discern the face of the sky; but can ye not discern the signs of the times?" (Matt. xvi. 3.) Clearly, then, the study of the times is not a blind thing, neither with-

out profit; even though it lead to cautionary
signals in most unexpected places.

"The times," — and what wonderful
times they are! Almost the "Arabian
Nights" in common life experience. "Many
run to and fro, and knowledge is increased."
With endless appliances for comfort, with
countless helps for work; and yet, if the
age must be named, it might well be called
"the Time of no time." For that is the universal, ceaseless complaint. Yet the days
are as long as ever; the sun "hasteth" no
faster "unto his going down;" each minute rings out its full round value; while the
ease of living is a thousand fold increased;
and still nobody has (or thinks he has) leisure to draw one long, calm, satisfying
breath, and to "eat his bread with quietness." Hezekiah thought *his* days flew "like
a weaver's shuttle;" but only steam rates
can describe ours. "Too busy!" — "No

time!" is the cry on every hand : the wide-spread reason, answer, and excuse. What has become of the self-controlled patience which two generations ago could wait a week for the mail, and contemplate a six months' voyage to the Sandwich Islands? or spend eight days on a sailing vessel between New York and Albany? The men of this generation would chafe to death before they reached Poughkeepsie. People do not appear to enjoy their breathlessness : one is reminded of the words of the Prophet : " Thou hast multiplied the nation, and not increased the joy ;" for everybody says, " How I would like to do this or that if only *I had time!* " Therefore much satis-faction does not seem to be crowded in. What is crowded out?

Church services, for one thing. Listen to your Wednesday-evening combination bell, and hear what it says. It is not so

very long since that bell had much more to
do. At nine o'clock Sunday morning came
Sunday school, with a Bible class or two in
the church gallery. Then service at half
past ten, Sunday school again at two (with
other Bible classes and outside mission
schools), church service at three, prayer
meeting at seven. During the week, prayer
meeting Tuesday night, lecture Thursday
night, teachers' meeting Saturday night.
And we no more thought of accepting any
other invitation for church nights, than we
thought (in those innocent days) of going
to the theatre or playing cards. And truly
we had small need. Ah, how good the
meetings were! How pleasant it was, as
one and another of many who now walk in
white beyond the flood, came softly into the
little room, — elders, deacons, "young men
and maidens, old men and children," — and
we all rose and sang together, —

> " Sweet and solemn be the season
>   When the friends of Jesus meet," —

a hymn I never hear sung nowadays.

> " Time is precious; we 'll improve it.
>   Worldlings talk of worldly things.
>   Leave the world to those who love it ;
>   'T is not thence our comfort springs.
>   Jesus owns us ;
>   Jesus is the King of kings."

I think I shall hardly hear " Zion " sung, to the end of my life, without those words chiming in.

Perhaps just at that time Dr. Skinner was going through Colossians, in a familiar, Bible-reading sort of way; pausing over such words as " puffed up," — or " after the rudiments of the world, and not after Christ," — and then the little company parted, with the benediction on their hearts. It was not only Time you had there, but Eternity as well.

As Charles Lamb's sister said of other
past pleasures, "We might do such things
now; but *do* we?" No; one night in the
week is all we can spare, and Sunday
services must be shortened. We are
too tired to get to church before eleven
o'clock, and really "a man ought to be
able to say what he has to say in twenty
minutes."

We think of the knights of old, that they
must have been strong to carry their armour; but what degree of force and endur-
ance enabled the men — and women — of a
hundred years ago, to sit out a two hours'
sermon in a perfectly cold church, with
hard seats and a New England winter?
I like long sermons myself; and being lin-
eally descended from those very people,
can "give a gay guess" how it was; but
what would have become of the people who
demand the aforesaid twenty minutes in

furnace heat ? Four verses of a hymn (or three) where once it was sung straight through, and prayers cut down to the general feeling of hurry ? To be sure, a little time may be saved by buying a newspaper on the way to church; by a moment's consultation in the porch ; by studying the shop windows on the way home, — windows now left obligingly at least half open. In this way the waste Sunday hours may help arrange plans for Monday. Perhaps you think this cutting-down process has been good for the ministers; but I doubt even that. Time and strength may indeed be set free for popular lectures and scientific books and after-dinner speeches; but I think the prayer meetings were better.

Who keeps up now the old Monthly Concert of prayer for the conversion of the world? except indeed the far-off missionaries, or some country church which has not found out how the world moves, but only that it is not yet converted?

Then family prayers. — But that is too long a subject for the end of a chapter.

CROWDED OUT.

IN a certain mansion of ten servants, where once I was much at home, the waiter (a dusky West Indian) used to declare emphatically, "Dere's no *time* for prayers in a house like dis." If he was right, then manifestly something else was wrong. But how many houses "like this" (in *that*) are built up now-a-days? What proportion of even the homes of church members bear the motto of another dwelling which also I knew well, — "For God, the Church, and the family"? Yet this last was one of the most blessed and blessing abodes this earth ever saw; and "Godliness *is* profitable for the life that now is."

Who really believes it, — in even small
household affairs "seeking first the kingdom"? Who prays with missionary Good-
ell, that not only his house, but "all the
furniture, may be consecrated"? Nay, if
we can get it fashioned like our neighbour's,
we are most of us content. People are out
of breath in the race, but it is not the race
described by Paul. He that striveth for
that mastery "is temperate in all things;"
and even his business knows its place.

Dr. Bickersteth said to me once that
women make an idol of their work; but
surely not the women alone. Does not the
shapeless thing crowd everybody, in every
place, with a right of way which is alto-
gether heathen? Take this one matter
of family prayer, — and setting aside the
houses where it has been quite crowded
out, to how many prosperous business men
(as to one I heard of) might come his

child's innocent comment, — " Father, my
teacher says we ought n't to say our prayers
fast." The bath is enjoyed, the toilet is
elaborate; the breakfast, if not lingered
over, yet has full justice. But the prayers
are hurried. Want of thought brings lack
of realization. The head of the house is
too well to remember: " The Lord killeth
and maketh alive," — too competent, to
recollect: " It is the Lord that giveth thee
power to get wealth." The morning paper
has told him of a rise in stocks, the barom-
eter hints at a change in the weather ; and
he is on the spring to meet and prevent or
take advantage, as the case may be. But
the tired look on his wife's face, which her-
alds for her a weary day ; the fretfulness of
a child who has got up " wrong foot first;"
some new — or old — fault in a servant, — all
these he will leave behind so soon, that they
are hardly worth praying about. Rather he

anticipates the joyful slam of the front door, which for eight hours at least will shut them off from him, and him from them.

As little, very often, does he realize what lies *outside* the door: the possible snares for his feet in the busy haunts down town, the lurking dangers that may await him in his office. "Infernal machines," truly, but not of a sort to be handed over to the police. Only believing prayer can thwart them, but that can.

How lovely, how fitting, then, that the householder should place all these varied interests in safe keeping before he goes! asking not only a blessing on basket and store, but also pleasant paths for the mother's feet and safe steps for the children. I fancy it would comfort many a wife's heart to hear her husband pray over *her* daily cares. And instead of vague generalities ("that we may not leave undone those

things which ought to be done"), he need
not be ashamed to come out boldly, and
pray for himself too, that he also may walk
this day " in the paths of righteousness "
" Set a watch, O Lord, before my mouth"
(Ps. cxli. 3). " Hold thou me up, and I shall
be safe " (Ps. cxix. 117).

And if not only for the circle at home
but also for the throng abroad he should
breathe a petition, — for his business associ-
ates, his workpeople, or those under whom
he serves, — if from every Christian household there went up, morning by morning,
such ascending prayers : O, what descend-
ing dews of grace would follow! How
sweetly and easily would the father go about
his toil and the mother to her labours, their
feet " shod with the preparation of the gospel of peace." What straight paths would
open before the business men, what safe es-
capes before the tempted ; what roots of

patience, what fruits of righteousness, would
spring up and grow and flourish ! Life so
transferred with a full heart to the Lord's
keeping is lifted at once out of the low
plane of mere making money and directing
servants, as also from the dead level of
incessant toil. A sense of God's unseen
legion makes us strong, the fresh breath
of his presence keeps down the dust ; and
all this poor rough-and-tumble world is
changed. How can we be angry with a
man in the afternoon, for whom we have
eagerly prayed in the morning ? How chafe
over difficulties, failures, remembering always, "It is the Lord"? Failures, did I say ?
in such a life no failure is possible.

"He always wins who sides with God."

But too often it is hurry in the morning
(or no prayers at all), and at night six-
o'clock dinners, seven-o'clock dinner-par-

ties ; the servants in a press, the children gone to bed. Or a visitor rings at the door, and nobody dare ask him to wait (*unless* for an incomplete toilet) or better still, will ask him in to join the family service.

But, say you, he is a gay young man ; he would not like it. Now as a rule, I think young men like (or like to witness) anything that is *real.* Or you think the visitor " does not believe in anything," — then it is time he should know there are people who *do.* One should not *obtrude* even the best· things. But if the prayer hour were as fixed as the hour for dinner, one might as properly invite in a stranger to the one as to the other ; he having in either case the right to refuse. I shall never forget the pleasure, when after a long summer drive to breakfast at a certain house, we found that the family had waited our arrival, and we all had prayers together before the meal

was served. Too many feel just the other
way. "We must have prayers a little early,
before they come," — or "a little late, after
they go."

Then as to the children. It is maybe
better for their health (and doubtless for
their complexions) to have their bread and
milk, and go to bed with only a far-off
whiff of the six-o'clock roast ; and you cannot well have prayers *before* that early
hour, for the head of the house is not at
home. But as I look back to my own
childish days, I would not, at a venture, give
up the prayer-time lessons, even for some-
what more of strength and colour. The
whole picture comes back to me now. The
little one of the house, nestled close to her
who had taken the mother's place ; the
elder girl sitting apart in dignified erect-
ness ; the servants, with folded hands and
reverent faces ; the weary seamstress, come

for a breath of refreshment after the many stitches of the day. I am afraid to go on, and tell what the clock said ! —

Children need health of mind as well as of body; and neither can flourish in nursery shade. I was reading lately of some one who had questioned many people as to the time and means of their conversion ; and Dr. Taylor's answer is a whole book of practical wisdom. "He did not know," he said : "he just grew up into it." Ah, I have seen such families, but they are not common. "Our sons as plants grown up in their youth. Our daughters as corner stones, polished after the similitude of a palace " (Ps. cxliv. 12).

But how often do you find that straight, vigorous growth of young men ; filling the world with fresh leafage, with precious fruit ? Where do you see the young women becoming the strong bond of the house, and yet shining with all exquisite symmetry and finish? The boys are sent to a hot-house to be forced, the girls get their polish at the dancing-school.

Now a man may much better grant his children less money and more attention. My father was a professional man in very full practice; but he always found time to give us delightful breakfast talks: talks for which we children had to prepare ourselves, he giving out the subject before-hand. Simple subjects, such as we could understand; what if the study stretched our minds a little. "The bread-stuffs of the world," — "Pitch, tar, and turpentine," — or "The English Regalia." Sometimes a name in history, or a great fact, like "Magna Charta." Then we hunted and studied and brought forth all our learning; too happy when we found some little detail which even our father did not know. We told, — and he corrected and organized our crude knowledge. And after tea, unless some *very* pressing case was on hand, he always read aloud to us for an hour. Or we studied engravings together, — or turned over books of etchings ; the youngest then kneeling in a chair at his side. Yes, of course, "we ought to have been in bed," — but nothing will ever make me wish that we had ! —

"Prayer is the key of the morning, and the lock of night," says some old writer : happy is the family whose day holds nothing which the one may not fitly open, and the other peacefully close.

"Happy is the people that is in such a case : yea, happy is the people whose God is the Lord " (Ps. cxliv. 15).

A TIME FOR EVERYTHING.

"TO everything there is a season, and a time to every purpose under the heaven," said the Preacher. But if *a* time, then also *time:* time for everything.

I shall be met here with a great shout of derision. As if anybody ever had time for anything in this workaday world? And if I go further, and say that when not it is our own fault; and that our Master in heaven never gives his servants more to do than they can do thoroughly; people will hold up hands at my ignorance. Well, I have lived as busy a life as most, and I repeat my words. Look at it. Half-done work is a thing the Lord cannot away with : the finish of creation is as marvellous as its vastness. Fuller and fuller grows the world of life, the deeper in you go ; but also more exquisite grows each detail. Finer and finer draws out the sting point of a wasp, under your more and more powerful magnifiers ; while the smallest needle man ever made, turns by degrees into a blunt crow-bar. The unsuspected carvings on a fish scale are dainty beyond description : the white chalk dust contains microscopic globes of spun silver, surpassing anything that Tiffany's most cunning workmen see even in their dreams. The little Mellicerta — to the naked eye as large as an ordinary full stop — has a mould upon its chin wherein it makes bricks from the muddy ditch water of its surroundings ; and builds to itself thereof a round tower of habitation or defence. The minute creature has no hands ; but deftly turning itself now this way, now that,

adroitly and accurately dumps out the finished brick on whichever spot of its wall
needs heightening or repair.

"O Lord, how manifold are thy works! in
wisdom hast thou made them all: the earth
is full of thy riches " (Ps. civ. 24).

You may see here — and in countless
like instances — what satisfies that all-
cognizant eye. You understand now what
the words in Genesis mean: " And God
saw everything that he had made, and,
behold, it was very good " (Gen. i. 31).

Man only left the perfect scheme, and
went on and " sought out many inventions."
Yet the rule is not changed : the measure to
which man should attain has never been cut
down. And so the Lord's servants must
not even " look back" from the plough ;
must have "every thought in captivity unto
Christ;" must " serve him with a perfect
heart ;" loving the Lord their God with

"all the heart and soul and mind and strength."

Is it likely then, that he will so arrange their lives that the service thus rendered shall be after all only job-work, — crude, imperfect, hurried through? Will he whose "tender mercies are over all his works," make his people only "to serve with rig-our"? Or is it probable that the great King whose "chariots are thousands of angels," and his messengers "an innumerable company," should constantly drive his poor human servants to distraction? It was under Pharaoh the Israelites had no time to breathe, — not under God.

No, the whole Bible denies it. And while they like other children of Adam must eat bread in the sweat of the brow, for them only falls the cool shadow on all the way of toil; and they only know that "man doth not live by bread alone."

3

So it may be, so it should be. You will find, if you search it out, that we are helping build " treasure cities " for Pharaoh, when our lives are " bitter " with every day's " brick and mortar:" it is by *his* taskmasters we are driven; and " bricks without straw" is the wearisome stint. The feverish haste and unchristian worry; the perpetual effort to do what we cannot, to seem what we are not, to have what we may not, — is it not like the old days of the bondage? " The people sighed" then — and they sigh now! yet the struggle keeps on. Be as rich as your neighbours, be dressed like your friends; go where they go, do what they do; hear all the preachers, sit on all the committees, serve on all the boards; trim all the dresses, decorate everything that can (or can *not*) be decorated. Anything, to keep the blood up to fever heat.

But, you say, these things are good, necessary, and useful. In moderation. But not for you, if they crowd your life and overset your nerves : so doing them, you help neither your friends nor the world. Better three quiet minds on a committee, than a dozen weary, hurried souls. Better the plainest bonnet, crowning a fresh, cheerful face ; or the commonest dress, borne hither and thither with swift elastic motions ; than all the triumphs of needlework, trailed round on languid feet. Better to take all preachers but your own on trust, and rest yourself with a book instead of a lecture.

Now indeed you hear all the lectures, but have no time for reading ; neither to "keep up" your music — yet you attend all the concerts. No leisure, it may be, to teach the children and answer their questions, because you are so very busy ruffling their frocks! The home farm grows up to weeds, while the farmer debates over ensilage. Or if you are one of those happy people who can be in twenty places at once, you will by and by pay for the distinction with overwrought nerves and broken strength. I have seen a woman rush from an ordination in New Jersey to a luncheon in New York, thence to a May anniversary; and thence — dear me, I do not know whither! Perhaps by the night train to a farewell missionary meeting in Boston.

But, you insist again, such things *are* right: some people's work, other people's play. Do then whatever right things you can do thoroughly, peacefully, and with no undue crowding of hands or heart; the best things first. An extra sermon you are too weary to take in, even from the preacher of the world, will not profit you much: witness Eutychus. A missionary meeting that unfits you for mission work at home, is worse than useless. How often we can guess the fatigue of our friends, from their irritability ; and maybe hear (or use) the sorrowful excuse : " Forgive me, — I did not mean to speak so, — but I am so tired ! " Manifestly there is here some great mistake. I do not believe it is the Lord's pleasure that his people should live in a perpetual rush and hurry. The whole teaching of *his* work is against it. Leaf by leaf the forest clothes itself with verdure ; with slightly quickened action sometimes after unavoidable delays, but never with any haste that mars its perfection. And from the time when the dayspring first "knew its place," a steady "more and more" has been the only rule of the morning.

" Yea, the stork in the heaven knoweth her appointed times, and the turtle and the

crane and the swallow observe the time of
their coming" (Jer. viii. 7).

The wren appears by the last of April,
and the catbirds on the tenth of May.
Absolute, regular order, without pressure,
without delay, is the law of the natural
world. And in revelation it is the same.
The very crown of Christian life in the
Bible is to be "always abounding," and yet
at rest: everything being adjusted with
that wonderful poise and balance which
is at the antipodes of all breathlessness,
hurry, and confusion. A soul "dwelling
at ease;" a heart "quiet from fear of evil;"
abiding in the shadow of a great peace.

> "A faith that shines more bright and clear
> When tempests rage without ;
> That even in danger feels no fear,
> In darkness knows no doubt."

And that even in the face of imminent need,
can "both hope, and quietly wait for the
Lord."

" Consider the lilies, how they grow "
(Matt. vi. 28).

" Better is an handful with quietness,
than both the hands full, with travail and
vexation of spirit " (Eccl. iv. 6).

Quietness indeed is the watchword of
these old Bible saints : "in quietness and
in confidence" is all their "strength." Thus
they are "diligent in business" — but
also "study to be quiet:" "serving God
day and night," yet "casting all their care
upon him :" "redeeming the time," and
still taking "no thought for the morrow."
The lilies themselves grow not more softly
and surely to their fragrant bloom ; the
birds of the air do not more simply and
unquestioningly live by the hourly rule :

" That thou givest them, they gather "
(Ps. civ. 28).

It may be more yesterday and less to-
day ; it may be now dainties, and then but

daily bread: yet all coming "from the good hand of our God upon us," they have learned "in whatsoever state" they are, "therewith to be content."

Thus they "eat their bread with joy," and their daily path is "by the waters of quietness." They "do their work with quietness," — they "lead a quiet and peaceable life;" and wear "the ornament of a meek and quiet spirit."

These are not the prevailing fashions of the day, even among church members. Look at the restless eyes, the anxious faces: note the dull murmur of unsatisfied desire, swelling every now and then into absolute complaint. Hear the Christian women worry over their housekeeping: see the up-town religious man at the down-town Exchange. Hat pushed back, coat thrown open, eyes wild, hands outstretched, voice uplifted; shouting, gesticulating, grasping, with the rest.

" My brethren, these things ought not so to be " (Jas. iii. 10).

Should " a good soldier of Jesus Christ " put off his uniform and wear a common dress, that he may make a better bargain? Or "an Israelite indeed" be ever seen without the "ribband of blue," the royal colours? "Ye shall wear it," said the Lord, "that ye may remember and do all my commandments, and be holy unto your God " (Num. xv. 40).

In a great Ward school which I visited once, you could pick out the Jewish children, all over the room, by the little closed mouths and silent lips when the praises of Jesus were sung. Ah, why will not people be as true to the true as they are to the false! For just so, should a believer be known, even on 'Change, as no worshipper of mammon, no truster in " uncertain riches." What though, like the three

in Babylon, he must stand alone, while all
the rest of the world are on their knees
before the golden image.

"Let your moderation be known unto
all men" (Phil. iv. 5).

"Walk as children of light" (Eph. v. 8).

Is it only "a woman's view"?   But
there surely must be a righteous way of
doing righteous things, — and the *un*righteous should as surely be let alone.   If that
also is a woman's view, it would take a wise
man to dispute it.   Let the dwellers at
home too remember this.   For how should
a Christian woman fret? even over dust
and unfaithful service.

"I beseech you by the meekness and
gentleness of Christ" (2 Cor. x. 1).

They are genuine annoyances, these
things: the host of trifling items in our
daily life which *ought* to be different: the
bad fitting of a dress, the imperfections

of a cook, the stupidity of a messenger;
not to speak of the unreasonableness which
now and then crops out in a friend. We
have (and should have) an honest dislike
to them all. Set them straight if you can,
— if a few wise words will do it.

" Ye which are spiritual restore such an
one in the spirit of meekness " (Gal. vi. 1).

But if not, take a long breath of silence
and press on. " The talk of the lips tend-
eth only to penury:" both of time and
patience. You may soon outstrip the
grievance, if you will but leave it where it
belongs, by the wayside. Stop to wonder
and complain, and it will spring to your
shoulders like Sindbad's old man of the
sea, and ride you all the day. The mis-
chievous insect horde can do little to hurt
a plant that is in full rich growth; with
head in the sunshine, and roots struck deep
" by the rivers of water."

I have called them trifles—for trifles they
are, in a world of life and death and souls
of men; but even in the face of much more
serious evils, still " Vor-warts ! " — as the
German officer said, with kindly quiet firm-
ness, when his little troop faltered before a
hail of bullets.

" Have not I commanded thee ?   Be
strong and of a good courage" (Josh. i. 9).

" Doe the nexte thynge," — and wait for
the next but one till it comes ; letting
neither the good of something you long for,
nor the disagreeableness of something you
wish well over, flurry your spirits.   Walk
round Jericho thirteen times, if need be,
but take also for that the allotted hours.   If
you crowd into one day the work marked
out for seven, you will be too much out of
breath to shout when the time comes, and
the walls will maybe never fall.

" By faith the walls of Jericho fell down,

after they were compassed about seven days " (Heb. xi. 30).

" Behold, the husbandman waiteth for the precious fruit of the earth, and hath long patience for it, until he receive the early and latter rain " (Jas. v. 7).

And we, poor blunderers, think one rain might do; planting our little seeds deep, and our great ones on the surface; and the length of *our* patience is not worth measuring. We think everything that will grow, must grow at once.

Yes, patience does seem very " long " sometimes ; and " after many days " looks far away: but it will come,—and the weary toiler shall return, " bringing his sheaves with him." Sheaves from many. an unnoted field, trophies from many an unrecorded battle ; all won, through the grace of God, by " patient continuance."

Then give everything the full time it

needs for perfect development. Be as
eager as you like, but keep all restless
hurry out of your heart and tongue and life:
it is the sure cause of many failures, many
mistakes. In his haste, David called "all
men liars" (Ps. cxvi. 11), ready to say no one
could be trusted. Worse than that, his flurried spirit thought God had forgotten him.

"I said in my haste, I am cut off from
before thine eyes" (Ps. xxxi. 22).

"Seest thou a man hasty in his words?
there is more hope of a fool than of him"
(Prov. xxix. 20).

And the rule goes deeper than mere
speech. "Be not hasty in thy spirit to
be angry" (Prov. vii. 9). "If there is any
occasion," adds the human proverb, "you
will have time enough."

Do you think I would have an easy-
going, slack-handed race of people? Not
so: they are to be not only "diligent in

business," but also "fervent in spirit;" with the genial glow which goes with all wholesome action.

"The king's business requireth haste" (1 Sam. xxi. 8).

Even Gabriel had to "fly swiftly," to be in time. "Run, speak to this young man," said one angel to another in the days of Zechariah. But the Bible haste is utterly unlike our hurry, and means only this: the utmost speed that consists with the most perfect going, and the least possible delay. It never means more, nor less: the "how" is never merged in the "when."

"I will run the way of thy commandments" (Ps. cxix. 32).

It is the daily rule. But so also is this:

"Ponder the path of thy feet" (Prov. iv. 26).

"The prudent man looketh well to his going" (Prov. xiv. 15).

"The wisdom of the prudent is to understand his way" (Prov. xiv. 8).

Being all summed up in one other word:

"My soul followeth hard after thee" (Ps. lxiii. 8).

"I made haste, and delayed not, to keep thy commandments" (Ps. cxix. 60).

There is plenty of such running in the Bible: quickened steps from quickened powers and a heart astir. Thus Abraham, with three heavenly guests to entertain, "hastened into the tent to Sarah," and then "ran unto the herd." Thus Aaron, when the sin-invited plague had broken out among the people, caught up his censer, "and ran into the midst of the congregation," and "stood between the dead and the living." The wife of Manoah "made haste and ran" to find her husband, that he too might hear the heavenly message; and David, with his five smooth stones, "hasted and ran" to meet the Philistine, the staff of whose spear was "like a weaver's beam." Elijah, at the word of the Lord, outstripped the king's chariot, — the father in the parable ran "a great way" to meet his repentant son ; and the disciples at Lystra "ran in" to restrain the crowd who were sounding *their* praises. But these were all cases of legitimate, well-ordered haste ; and so the actors moved under the shadowing of the promise :

"When thou runnest, thy foot shall not stumble" (Prov. iv. 12).

Nay more, of this :

"They shall run, and not be weary" (Is. xl. 31).

No mistakes, no confusion, were possible.

"I therefore so run,"—said Paul, — "not as uncertainly" (1 Cor. ix. 26).

They followed the Lord so close, that there was no doubt which way he was

4

leading; and they went as fast as he led them.

Yes, "haste," "speed," "run," are good Bible words, with an urgent Bible meaning; but it is only such glad pressure as the sun is in, which moment by moment, and without the loss of a single one, "hasteth to his place whence he arose." There is all the difference in the world between the haste which comes from crowding, and that which springs forward with intense consecration to the work in hand; saying, for the time: "This one thing I do."

Everything in the Bible is against our feverish rush. The good seed in the good ground, with its vigorous, ceaseless, fruitful growth, is compared with those who "having heard the word, keep it, and bring forth fruit with patience."

"First the blade, then the ear, after that the full corn in the ear" (Mark iv. 28).

It is so in nature, it is so in grace; it should be so in every department of human life. " Let thy garments be alway white" — even " unspotted," — but how can that be, if you rush through this muddy world at such breakneck speed ? Take the simple Bible image : Christ's flock are " led," "guided," "shepherded ;" and through differing little paths they follow on ; pausing to feed, stopping to rest, drinking "of the brook in the way." The rush and confusion come only when they are drawn off from their Shepherd by some sudden allurement, or are frightened away by some foolish dread. As if He did not know ! — as if He would not take care !

Do you ever wait to make sure the Lord is before you, in those ways you tread so rapidly ? You hurry in, not thinking ; you hurry on, not looking ; and thus many a thing is done which should not (and other-

wise would not) be ; while many another is
neglected ; and the same excuse is spread
over all : want of time. No leisure to
study your plans by the light of the Bible-
lamp ; too driven to keep your temper : in
the mêlée how often patience goes down,
and meekness, and sometimes truth.

"What shall I render to the Lord for all
his benefits toward me ?" (Ps. cxvi. 12.)

Shall it be a life like that ?

Nay, it is all wrong, — all the greatest
mistake : for I do verily believe that this
high pressure is quite our own fault. I
believe that nothing need be neglected
in the busiest life : nothing which the
Lord has given us to do. Idleness has
no room there : neither work *not* given :
neither unhelpful play : and it is when
we let in one or all of these, that we
get hurried, worried, and out of breath.
For arrears are always hard to meet ; the

only way with time as with money is to keep out of debt. Like Jane Taylor's discontented pendulum, we must learn that however many ticks we can think of in a second, or may execute in a year, there is always given for each the moment to tick in. And if the clock stands steady, and the pendulum hangs true, every tick will have its full, round proportions, and mark off its atom of finished work. So shall the "fulness of time" take its place with "the patience of hope," and "the labour of love."

THE TANGLED SKEIN.

IN the old fairy tale, a young girl is set down to her embroidery before a great heap of tangled silk. Skeins of every colour, of every shade, are there; but all mixed, twisted, snarled, in hopeless confusion. A fair pattern lies there too: a pansy, a "heartsease;" and from the heap of confusion she must draw all her materials with . which to work a perfect copy of the flower of peace. And she gazes from one to the other, and drops her hands in despair. Like this, it seems to me, looks many a life : and even so hangs many a hand, that has countless exquisite shining threads within its reach. The material is ready, the pattern is given; and yet confusion rules, and perplexity reigns, and there is little "fruit to perfection." All the fine powers and possibilities are knotted and clogged; a strand of blue ends abruptly in a tangle of yellow; or red is twined in until the whole thing looks purple. Yet there lies the calm-faced pattern, to shew what may be done; and before it many a poor worker breaks down in tears. And then comes in the cunning temptation to give up matching colours *exactly*, and after a pull at the right, to take instead an easier-running thread of wrong. What we in our very incorrect phrasing, call "doing the best we can." The white thread is in a knot, — catch up a gray one and work with that: the blue is tangled — make shift with the purple. But you can never work out heartsease so.

In the story, nothing brought the distracting mass to terms, but the wand of the fairy Order ; and only Christian order can ever smooth out our life task; making the threads run clear and even, working out the plan, enabling us to say at the end : "I have fought a good fight ; I have finished my course ; I have kept the faith."

Christian order: the counsel, the guiding, the touch, of Him who "telleth the number of the stars," and "calleth them all by their names" (Ps. cxlvii. 4). Out of darkness and silence and seething mist, came forth at his word the endless harmonies of nature ; and chaos passed into a world of regular development, lit up with colour, beautified with form, full of hidden wealth and untold forces ; and yet through all :

> " With never a leaf or a blade too mean
> To be some happy creature's palace."

Like that I would wish my life to be, — with all least things, as all greater ones, doing their sweet work ceaselessly, from day to day. The duties joys, the minutes golden; the life course no longer a tormenting maze or a disheartening hurry, but what every one's life should be: the clear working out of "a plan of God." How good, how blessed, how grand, *his* plan — for the least of us — is sure to be ; enfolding for each the very best possibilities, the very highest results of which that one is capable.

And in what region of earth, do you ask, could such constant success be possible? Just here where you stand. "The word is very nigh thee." And no one could ever miss it, were only "He spake, and it was done" the rule of the human as of the material creation. The best cure, the only sure preventive, of confusion, worry, and failure, lies in the simple Bible words:

"Whatsoever he saith unto you, do it" (John ii. 5).

Choose so heartily the Lord's will concerning yourself and all other things, that to know that shall be your only question. Claim his promise : " I will guide thee with mine eye " (Ps. xxxii. 8).

And then, " be not as the horse or as the mule, whose mouth must be held in with bit and bridle ; " but " understanding what the will of the Lord is," be ready with the answer : " Here am I : send me " (Is. vi. 8). Having asked him to lead, then follow. When he bids you " depart far hence unto the Gentiles," go ; however much you would like to stay and preach to the people at home. Or if he says : " Return unto thine own house, and tell how great things the Lord hath done for thee," do that too : even though you might greatly prefer to be " with him " in more distinguished places. Even if in the midst of an avalanche of work he calls you " apart into a desert place to rest awhile,"—and even if the desert mean only a headache or a rainy day instead of a journey,—make no complaint, but follow close ; sure only that Christ is in the ship and will be upon the land whither you go for rest ; or it may be in the darkened room. Peter, "between two soldiers, bound with two chains," slept so sweetly, that he could hardly rouse up to see an angel.

Perhaps all the best churches are supplied,—perhaps all the regular classes have teachers, and there is nothing left for you but the driblets. I went through that experience once, and I know how it feels. Class after class was disposed of, until only the so-called poorest class remained : a little tangle of two or three very inconspicuous bits of humanity. The superintendent approached me with apologetic caution. " I don't know what to do," he said, hesitating.

"You see Miss —— refused that class, — so I had to give her another."

Well, I had not come there to "refuse" anything; although, being human like the rest, I did think the big Bible classes looked very pleasant. But I took my place; and soon found (as we always do) that where the Lord puts us, it is good to be. The superintendent however was not content; and when a few weeks later I was promoted (as he thought it) I went to my new duties with rather a sad heart. For one of my small hard-faced creatures got hold of my hand, and said: "I don't want you to go!" Sad and ashamed too, — that I could ever have had any thought but one, about work in the weediest corner, or on the dustiest highway. Like the then but half-converted disciple, so little absorbed in the mighty charge and question to myself, that I found time to ask, "Lord, and what shall this man do?" And Jesus answered him: "What is that to thee? follow thou me" (John xxi. 22). Promotion is rather a sharp-edged thing, when it makes you suddenly feel how many sizes too small you are for your present place.

In this world, filled to its last corner with work that should be done, one needs a very single eye, a very self-controlled hand, a very heaven-directed heart, to pick out just his own work and no other. For "the harvest truly is plenteous, but the labourers are few." And the time is short. There *is* time to accomplish what we have to do, but not an atom too much. The poor child in the story, weeping over her task, must yet finish it "before dinner," — and we also ours, before "the night cometh, wherein no man can work." There will be no chance for it later on. Yet all the more need is there to keep clear of confusion : to draw out the right working thread and have it run freely and without a hitch. And I know of no way like this : " Whatsoever he saith unto you, do it" (John ii. 5). " Ye shall not add unto the word which I command you, neither shall ye diminish from it, that ye may keep the commandments of the Lord your God, which I command you" (Deut. iv. 2).

Then you will not be tempted by the brilliant threads of scarlet that lie so close at hand: a pansy — not a poppy — is your allotted task. Work in lovingly and patiently the quiet blues and purples; and if from your flower all gayer tints are lacking, yet be not cast down. The darkest heartsease hath ever a golden eye ; and when the last stitches are in, you will know it too. "At evening time it shall be light."

" As God leads me, will I go,
  Nor choose my way.
  Let him choose the joy or woe
  Of every day.
  They cannot hurt my soul,
  Because in his control :
  I leave to him the whole, —
  His children may.

" As God leads me, I am still
  Within his hand :
  Though his purpose my self-will
  Doth oft withstand.
  Yet I wish that none
  But his will be done,
  Till the end be won,
  That he hath planned.

" As God leads me, so my heart
  In faith shall rest.
  Nor grief nor joy my soul shall part
  From Jesus' breast.
  In sweet belief I know,
  Which way my life doth go —
  Since God permitteth so —
  That must be best."

So living, you see at once no failure is possible, — neither can confusion creep in. Step-by-step following, is the most quieting, disentangling thing in all the world.

In the parable of the supper, the servants did not rush blindly on; but went and came, went and came, between their Master and their work. He knew what he wanted done, *they* wanted to do nothing else. And never people wrought with more close-knit efficiency; seeming as fresh at the end of their day's work as at the beginning. Fresher, in fact; for they went from "calling" to "bringing," and from that to "compelling;" but always with a, "Lord, it is done as thou hast commanded."

"They that wait on the Lord shall renew their strength" (Is. xl. 21).

For want of just that quiet onwaiting (as if the morning orders could cover all the day) we undertake rashly, drive on un-

wisely, make mistakes, stop to worry —
and then the work piles up. Now the
promise is: " I will instruct thee and teach
thee in the way which thou shalt go"
(Ps. xxxvi. 6).

Hour by hour, and step by step. No
tangle of difficulties shall then distress my
feet.

" I will lead them in paths they have not
known" (Isa. xlii. 16).

No night of confused uncertainty delay
my going.

" The darkness and the light are both
alike to thee " (Ps. cxxxix. 12).

Even the burden and heat of the day
shall not long weigh down my heart :

"I will be as the dew unto Israel" (Hosea
xiv. 5).

And the tumult of opposition must grant
me a safe passage through ; " for he knoweth all the fords."

"He bindeth the floods from overflowing" (Job xxviii. 1).

"The Lord sitteth upon the flood; yea, the Lord sitteth King for ever" (Ps. xxix. 10).

How easily and sweetly it follows then:

"The Lord will give strength unto his people; the Lord will bless his people with peace" (Ps. xxix. 11).

I do not like to hear of "overworked" Christians: it seems an anomaly. And as little should they ever dwell in confusion. Not that there will be no questions to ponder, no puzzles to see through: follow close as you may, you cannot know *until* you know, which way the Lord is leading. He may put the Red Sea before you, — he may suffer Pharaoh to overtake: or he may appoint you a long time of seemingly useless waiting. But there need be no unrest, no flurried thoughts.

" Great peace have they that love thy law, and nothing shall offend them " (Ps. cxix. 165).

" And so it was, when the cloud abode from even unto the morning, and the cloud was taken up in the morning, then they journeyed: whether by day or by night that the cloud was taken up, they journeyed. Or whether it were two days, or a month, or a year, that the cloud tarried upon the tabernacle, remaining thereon, the children of Israel abode in their tents, and journeyed not : but when it was taken up, they journeyed. At the commandment of the Lord they rested in their tents, and at the commandment of the Lord they journeyed " (Num. ix. 21–23).

For the prayer of Israel in their right minds, is ever :

" If thy presence go not with me, carry us not up hence " (Ex. xxxiii. 15).

Absolutely sure then to work out the old blessed experience of the Lord's daily care:

"Who went before you, to search you out a place to pitch your tents in" (Deut. i. 33).

Marching under the triumphant standard of unnumbered fights, which never yet a shot could pierce nor weather stain.

"Jehovah-nissi" (Ex. xvii. 15).

"His banner over us" is "love" (Cant. ii. 4).

And on *that* flag, most truly, "the sun never sets."

"The Lord is my shepherd : I shall not want" (Ps. xxiii. 1).

You see how easy it is to be quiet from fear of evil: you see how in so simply straightforward a life there can be little real perplexity. The Lord will indeed " be inquired of for this," but then he will hear.

"David enquired of the Lord, saying, Shall

I go up into any of the cities of Judah?
And the Lord said unto him, Go up. And
David said, Whither shall I go up? And
he said, Unto Hebron " (2 Sam. ii. 1).

It is as simple as that.

" If any of you lack wisdom, let him ask
of God" (Jas. i. 5).

We may need to pray:

" Lead me in a plain path, because of
mine enemies " (Ps. xxvii. 1).

" Make thy way straight before my face "
(Ps. v. 8).

But the answer is sure: " The meek will
he guide in judgment " (Ps. xxv. 9).

"In all thy ways acknowledge him, and
he shall direct thy paths " (Prov. iii. 6).

" Cause me to know the way wherein I
should walk," — cries the troubled one.

And the promise is unfailing :

" The Lord shall guide thee continually "
(Is. xxviii. 11).

"And thine ears shall hear a voice behind thee, saying, This is the way, walk ye in it, when ye turn to the right hand, and when ye turn to the left" (Is. xxx. 21).

But how many people nowadays have restful souls? — restful and resting. How many, like their Master, can sleep when there is "a great storm of wind," "a great tempest in the sea," and "the ship covered with the waves"? True, he knew that he could lay the tempest — but *they* know it too. "There shall no harm happen to the vessel wherein Christ is," wrote Samuel Rutherford: "but the crazed ship and the seasick passengers shall both get safe to land."

But remember the words with which we set out:

"Whatsoever he saith unto you, do it."

Faith is quite useless without obedience.

NOW.

ANOTHER plain and very disentangling rule (and a wonderful time-saver) is this:

"As we have therefore opportunity" (Gal. vi. 10).

O, what trouble comes by the disregard of it! For want of thought, or through mere supineness, the right moment for a word, a deed, slips by unheeded, and we tire ourselves out in the search for it again. Yesterday I could have given such a one a word of counsel, — to-day I have run all over town and cannot find him. Of course the proper work of to-day lies by meanwhile. Why did I not speak yesterday ?— probably

I was timid, or shy, or self-indulgent; and
now if I am mercifully allowed another opportunity, it can be but a second best.
Well for my uneasy conscience if both man
and opportunity have not drifted for ever
beyond my reach. To-day I can give a
little much-needed help: by to-morrow the
help may be useless, or my power gone;
or it will take twice the labour, with half the
success. The very fact that I held back
to-day, will put me at a disadvantage to-
morrow. Yesterday my violets would have
sweetened a sick-room, — to-day they are
withered. Why were they not sent yesterday? O, I was so busy. But to-day I
must first take time to find fresh ones, and
then maybe carry them all too late. The
pale sufferer has gone where "everlasting
spring abides," and I have lost my chance.
The working thread which is manageable
as the Lord presents it, becomes knotted

and twisted with a dozen more, by our neglect.

Do you see why we are to be "instant"— on the alert — " in season, out of season "? wide awake to seize each swift-winged moment, " buying up opportunities." Eager to do *now* the Lord's bidding, because when by-and-by arrives, he will tell us something else. And remember, it is only now that anything can be done. We regret yesterday, we plan for to-morrow, but we must act to-day. And if ever a missed opportunity should again present itself, it will still be in the guise of an inexorable " now." " Turn ye now " (Jer. xxv. 5). " Prove me now " (Mal. iii. 10). While to those who slighted their opportunity, failed to use it, the Lord soon added : " Sleep on now, and take your rest " (Matt. xxvi. 45).

O loss, never to be forgotten nor made up. They might have watched with Christ

one hour, and they did not ! — No wonder
they were ready to forsake him and flee
when the test came : a neglected privilege
is a long step towards a committed sin.

Neither is there any enemy in front like
a forsaken duty in the rear. Israel refused
their first chance against Amalek ; and
then rushing up, out of time, found that
the Lord was not before them, and were
miserably discomfited. But the people who
obey exactly, and obey at once, are " strong
and very courageous ; " and they only "re-
deem the time."   For prompt obedience
leaves no margin of waste.   Not only you
have the right moment in which to do (and
everything is easier done then) but no time
is lost in after regrets, and sorrowful tears,
and prayers for forgiveness over slack-
handed delays. The eunuch was well on
the road before Philip got his orders ; and
Philip had to run to catch him ; and yet

the man was questioned, answered, converted, baptized, and Philip away again, before some of us would have decided whether the Lord had not better send another man to do the work. Andrew went for his brother the minute he thought of it; the other Philip drew Nathanael along as soon as he found him. The four men bring the palsied one between them, break up the roof, let him down, — and forthwith he walks away on his own feet, "carrying that whereon he lay;" and the four go off light-hearted and with hands ready for other work. Cornelius, bid to send for Peter, sent "immediately;" and "without gain-saying," "as soon as he was sent for," Peter came. "Whatsoever he saith unto you, that do:" both so, and *now*.

To men in that temper difficulties sink down into the common dust of the high-way: the roof, the distance, the unlikelihood, go for nothing. For our humility is too often sloth, and our prudence but just "the fear of man." "He that observeth the wind shall not sow; and he that regardeth the clouds shall not reap" (Eccl. xi. 4).

Remember how Moses displeased the Lord, by maintaining that he was not "eloquent," — not fitted for the work which the Lord gave him to do. Remember the "What doest thou here?" to Elijah, when he had fled away in despair from a false church and a persecuting world. What more *could* he do, among such a people? and yet:

"What doest thou here, Elijah?" (1 Kings xix. 9.)

Think of the time Jonah wasted, because he shrank from declaring to rich Nineveh "the whole counsel of God." He was sent with a message, and he would not deliver it.

It took months of experiences to bring him to his duty ; and then he had to take up the thing just where he had laid it down.

Then think of the lost days to Balaam, when having been told what to do (or rather what *not* to do) he set himself to get the orders reversed. Alas, it was more than lost time with him : it ended in lost eternity.

He had his reward.

" I will promote thee to great honour," said Balak: and Balaam forgot that " Shame shall be the promotion of fools " (Prov. iii. 35).

He tried to serve two masters, and pleased neither; sending away the first messengers when the Lord said, " Thou shalt not go." But when the second came, with bigger offers, he asked again ; and this time the Lord let him have his way. He got frightened sometimes as he jogged along ; saying,

"Now therefore if it displease thee, I will get me back again:" but still he went on; going sideways, and looking over his shoulder, yet holding on his "perverse way." With that strange fear which is not repentance, thinking something was after him, but failing even to imagine the drawn sword which glittered on ahead, until "the dumb ass reproved the prophet."

O what miserable temporizing and haggling we have over our orders sometimes! teasing until we get our "head," and then creeping along with a smiting "If it displease thee." And O what loss of time, strength, and comfort it entails!

"What thing soever I command you, observe to do it: thou shalt not add thereto, nor diminish from it" (Deut. xii. 32).

More than that:

"Whatsoever ye do, do it heartily" (Col. iii. 23).

But "heartiness" and hurry, like knowledge and wisdom, have "ofttimes no connection." In fact the very want of heartiness brings hurry.

"He also that is slothful in his work, is brother to him that is a great waster" (Prov. xviii. 9).

If the thing is hard, take hold at once; if there are difficulties, meet them now: letting the proper work of each minute fall into place as surely and sweetly as the minute itself ticks off. You can often do it and have done with it, while you are wishing you could do something else. I said work, — I should have said duty. For the required business of the hour may be sleep or rest instead of action; and must as little be slighted. Do that also with your might; and no more spoil your rest with work, than your work with idleness. Even the nerveless iron locomotive needs intervals of "cooling off:" the same engine does not take you from New York to Albany, but is switched off at Poughkeepsie for its turn of quiet. Time better spent so, than in costly repairs. The seasons of proper rest, of helpful study ("that the man of God may be perfect, thoroughly furnished unto all good works") are but the whetting of the sickle, the feathering of the arrow, for better and swifter work. How often are we laid by with a day's illness, just because in our self-willed zeal we have refused to take an hour of rest. Lay down your burden at the Lord's feet, O tired worker, and trust it there, until you are fit to take it up again. Can the great enemy of souls steal even one, from under *His* watching?

"There is that neither day nor night seeth sleep with his eyelids" (Eccle. viii. 16).

Cannot yours close at the proper time, leaving all to his almighty care?

Consider the lilies of the field, O women, toiling on into the night that the children's dresses may be finished. "Where is your faith?" Is it *service* to stitch your eyes out, and your brain into a whirl? Even in great things, the Lord himself put "to do the will of God," before "to finish his work." Yet people hurry along, bending under a dull weight of oppression, which they would not dare charge upon God, nor quite like— in heathen fashion — to lay upon fate; but least of all do they own it is Pharaoh. *Have* the children really no clothes? Yes, but not so fine as their neighbours'. *Must* you go to this meeting, half sick as you are? "No — but — Well, I do not want somebody else in my chair." — Ever so much of our over work is really self-indulgence. Are we bound to wear just such a dress, give just such a dinner, make just (or at least) so much money? No, by no righteous law, human or divine. It is Pharaoh's taskmasters, as I said. Try close, instant obedience to the Lord's hourly guiding, and see how the friction will die out, the confusion clear away. Perhaps you may not then find time to tie up the door-knobs in white muslin bags, — possibly a bargain may now and then escape you : but

"Better is an handful with quietness, than both the hands full with travail and vexation of spirit" (Eccle. iv. 6).

All the clear health of mind and body you can gather will not be too much, if you are to live like the woman of Proverbs xxxi. 10–31, the man of 2 Tim. vi. 11–15. Steady nerves and a calm brain are great backers of faith, in this world where the height of success is to be,

"Troubled on every side, yet not distressed; perplexed, but not in despair" (2 Co. iv. 8).

Truly, such a one is "a wonder unto many."

"His branches shall spread, and his beauty shall be as the olive tree, and his smell as Lebanon" (Hos. xiv. 6).

ALL THINGS FULL OF LABOUR.

I TALK of rest, I say you may be quit of confusion; but let not any one picture to himself a life with little to do, or even fancy that such a life would be pleasant. I suppose the busiest of us but faintly realize the things which might be done. The work lies all about you, even if you never take it up; but *if* you do not, your own personal loss is very great. You cannot make time so: you only kill it, lose it, throw it away.

"Occupy till I come," said our Master,— and that word searches out every corner of possibility: each hour is lent to see "how much every man will gain by trading;" not for himself, but for the great Owner of it all. What the Lord Jesus would have done we are to do, where he would have gone we are to go. And all with the prompt, joyful alacrity which marks those servants who not only "wait for their Lord," but also "love his appearing." While "a little more sleep, a little more slumber, a little more folding of the hands together," as surely tells that the servant saith in his heart: "My Lord delayeth his coming."

"Full of labour,"—but if you take it right, this "occupy" is also full of the richest, sweetest pleasure. The marginal reading of Eccle. i. 5 : "The sun panteth to his place whence he arose:" just describes, I think, the true wholesome state of a wholesomely living soul. That eager, glad, strained (but not *over*strained) endeavour after right ends ; never ceasing, never hurried : "rejoicing as a strong man to run a race."

"Shine like the sun in every corner," said George Herbert : the human translation of "Occupy till I come" (Lu. xix. 13).

But this joy in the thought of to-morrow's work, presupposes the work of to-day well done. If *that* has been left at loose ends, to be afterwards painfully caught up and knit together, we reach "the place whence we arose," panting after a very different sort : breathless, and tired ; for it makes all the odds in the world whether you pursue your business, or your business you. A pretty day the old clock would have had of it, if after idling over his work three quarters of an hour, he had tried to chink in all the neglected ticks ! Look at the indicators on the face of a day-and-month telling clock, and see how softly and irreversibly June changes to July, and the 1 into the 2. The time — the proper time — for one thing is gone, the time for another is come ; and there is not room for both. An impenetrability in things immaterial, as in the material, confronts us on every hand.

" To everything there is a season, and a time for every purpose under the heaven" (Eccle. iii. 1).

"A time to kill, and a time to heal; a time to break down, and a time to build up."

"A time to rend, and a time to sew ; a time to keep silence, and a time to speak " (Eccle. i. 3, 7).

Neither is there in action any more than in opinion a convenient middle ground which either side may use at will.

"He that is not with me is against me: and he that gathereth not with me scattereth " (Lu. xi. 23).

Whatever is not gain, is loss. We comfort ourselves over to-day's neglect, with, O I can do it to-morrow : forgetting that to-morrow also will have its own appointed duties, and not one minute to spare for the waste of to-day. And thus begins a system of borrowing time, at ruinous rates of interest.

It stands to reason then that no time must be squandered. In this as in everything throughout the natural world, the rule is absolute fulness, as close pressed as consists with absolute perfection : not a blade of grass too many, not a quarter inch too much. And so for us and our occasions there are minutes enough, but not one to throw away. Then of course it follows that each minute has its own appointed morsel of work ; and every minute that flits by unloaded, flings its proper burden on the rest. This is one great way in which we get in a hurry and keep in a hurry ; letting our work roll up like a snowball, until the separate light flakes become a mass too heavy to lift ; and flesh and heart too, break down in the attempt. But when all is said, the work remains : work ever increasing, never done. When we clear a lookout to the river among our cedars, for a little the open space rejoices our eyes ; and then directly, as if they had been waiting their chance, the trees on either side stretch out their branches, and close it in. You go to see one poor person, and you find three ; you sit down to mend one rent, and behold there are two. We wanted to give comfort and rest one summer to some city-fagged student with no hotel bills in his power ; and almost before we knew we had spoken our wish, *six* such students were offered us. All apparently waiting for just our one poor little room. It made us feel sore-hearted.

"All things are full of labour ; man cannot utter it" (Eccle. i. 8).

There is simply no end to the things to be done. Thorns and thistles grow here, and fields white for harvest stand there; and the sweat of the face is the daily experience. And Solomon goes on to state what to some of us is the hardest part of all: the wearisome sameness that comes in. If only some thistles could be yellow!— if only some thorns wore their prickles at the tips of the branches! if only the nettles would sting with a little change of sensation! Even a blue caterpillar would be a relief, and a green wire-worm rouse some faint sensation. But no:

"The thing that hath been, it is that which shall be; and that which is done, is that which shall be done: and there is no new thing under the sun" (Eccle. i. 9).

The same faults, the same needs, start up day in, day out; and from the time men first put on stockings, the holes have come in

the same places. Even the pleasure seekers
find it true, who spend their time in search-
ing for novelty. Life seems to take a certain area, within which the years swing back
and forth, pendulum fashion, and never go
beyond. It is one round of cooking, sweep-
ing, and mending, — or on the other hand,
of ordering dinners and guiding the house,
— or of dressing, visiting, driving to the
Park, and coming home. Either way it is
just a round.

"Is there anything whereof it may be
said, See, this is new?" (Eccle. i. 10.)

The same sins to fight, the same sorrows
to comfort, the same places to go to, the
same people to see. Men get a little variety
out of the rise and fall of stocks, the making and losing of money; the President
going in, and the President going out.
But even that, for the most part, subsides
into an average: it is but up and down,

four years and four years, when all is said.
There is little variety (or at least much
sameness) even for men. They hail the
same omnibus, catch the same train every
morning, nod to the same people on the
way, and come back to the same dinner
hour every night. Say about the same
thing to their wives at dinner, smoke the
same cigars, rustle the same newspapers,
stroll out for a half-hour in the same
streets, or drop in on the same cronies, to
discuss the same subjects. A bit of gos-
sip —a business report — the bulletin of the
weather, — nothing of much more refreshing power than the entries in the old
journal in the Spectator: "Mem: Grand
Vizier certainly hanged."

The elevated road made a small sensation for a while, and so will the balloon
express, — but it will not last. Solomon
called it a "sore travail" this machinery,

working with an endless band ; and looked at so, it is.

" What profit hath a man of all his labour which he taketh under the sun ?" (Eccle. i. 3).

" Generation passeth away, and generation cometh," — " the sun ariseth, and the sun goeth down ; — the wind goeth toward the south, and turneth about unto the north," — " all the rivers run into the sea," — and after all, " the sea is not full."

" All the labour of man is for his mouth, and yet the appetite is not filled " (Eccle. vi. 7).

" The eye is not satisfied with seeing, nor the ear with hearing " (Eccle. i. 8).

When we have seen this thing, let us hunt up something else ; when we have this, let us get the other. When our barns are full (note well the word) let us pull them down and build bigger. A restless sameness fills all the world ; and there is no hope, according to Solomon, that this state of things can ever be mended. It was all "vanity and vexation of spirit," to his sagacious mind. And even in the great facts of life and death he found the same monotony.

"All things come alike to all" (Eccle. ix. 2).

"As it happeneth to the fool, so it happeneth even to me" (Eccle. ii. 15).

The strange, humbling oneness of humanity crept under the royal robes, climbed up the ivory throne.

"Yea, though he live a thousand years twice told, yet hath he seen no good : do not all go to one place ? " (Eccle. vi. 6.)

"The house appointed for all living" (Job xxx. 23).

And from "dust to dust," walled in the longest life. Even so, Solomon could not get rid of them and their monotony.

" There is no end of all the people "
(Eccle. iv. 16).

" That which hath been is now, and that
which is to be hath already been " (Eccle.
iii. 15).

" An end of all perfection " David had
found, and easily ; but when Solomon
sought for the end of *im*perfection — alas,
it lay hid beneath the receding pointers
of the rainbow ! It was a melancholy view
enough.

" Is there taste in the white of an egg ? "
(Job vi. 6.)

And things are nearly as bad in our own
day. The monotony of labour in time-worn
channels, weighs down the race. The tree
of life, bearing " twelve manner of fruits,"
groweth not hereaway. Now as then,

" That which is crooked cannot be made
straight, and that which is wanting cannot
be numbered " (Eccle. i. 15).

And if even Solomon thought "of making many books there is no end," and found "much study" a weariness, what would he have said in our time?

"There is no end of all his labour; neither is his eye satisfied with riches" (Eccle. iv. 8).

"He that loveth silver shall not be satisfied with silver; nor he that loveth abundance with increase" (Eccle. v. 10).

Universal discontent follows on the heels of the universal hurry; and sameness and weariness go hand in hand. And which of us cannot smile and sigh too over that clause about the rivers, which sets forth in finer language what we say so often and so despairingly: "I never get through!" All the ceaseless work of the day, the week, the year, has been poured into that ocean of demand, — "yet the sea is not full." There will be just as much call to-morrow as there

is to-day. From work basket to mission
school, the work grows — not diminishes ;
and of necessity, for the most part, falls into
a gray routine.

Like the foam streaks on the river, which
sometimes for hours together show little
change of outline ; though wave after wave
rolls under them, and rolls away. Some
one has acutely defined " work " to be :
" *doing the same thing over;* " and we all
know how many a labour seems like play,
while it is new ; and many another presses
hard, just because it is old. The shoulder
is tired in just that place, the head is weary
of just that thought. Even in play it is
true. I knew a woman once into whose
young soul the monotony of life had pressed
so deep, that she every now and then, at
church, went up the aisle that was furthest
from her pew, " for a change ! " " I do wish
worsted dresses would come in fashion,"

she said to me one day. "I am so tired of wearing silk!"

We workers are better off than that, though we too feel the sameness; but there is some help in remembering that it must be so.

"While the earth remaineth, seedtime and harvest, and cold and heat, and summer and winter, and day and night, shall not cease" (Gen. viii. 22).

In all the great features, one year will be like another, while the world stands. Neither will to-day ever be able to do yesterday's work, or to-morrow's work; and when we try that, or expect that, we easily grow discouraged, and make labour indeed a curse. But to-day will always be full.

Once a year the old Israelites were to eat the Passover, staff in hand and shoes on feet; but to us is given the hourly rule:

"Let your loins be girded about, and your lamps burning" (Lu. xii. 35).

For even after a hard day's work the call may sound :

"Gird thyself, and come forth and serve me" (Lu. xvii. 9).

The minute-men of the Christian Commission even slept in full preparedness for action, ready at any moment to spring up and go. And there may suddenly rage a battle within your hearing, there may come wounded within your reach. You have already perhaps done much, but now do more: no putting off of armour while the war holds on. By and by, when the long life-day has sunk to rest, it shall be said :

"Go and sit down to meat."

"Blessed are those servants whom the Lord when he cometh shall find watching : verily I say unto you, that he shall gird himself, and make them to sit down to meat, and will come forth and serve them " (Lu. xii. 37).

"The time came that the saints possessed the kingdom " (Dan. vii. 12).

Then, when there shall be no more "wars, nor rumours of wars:" then, when there shall be "time no longer;" this ever coming, ever going, succession of hours and days and months and years, where before we can name the present it is already past. No more escaping opportunities, and possibilities that start up and fly: no more lives that sink down "as a shadow that declineth."

> "No rude alarms of raging foes;
> No cares to break the long repose;
> No midnight shade, no clouded sun,
> But sacred, high, eternal noon."

No need then to say one to another: "Know the Lord; for all shall know him, from the least of them unto the greatest of them " (Jer. xxxi. 34).

No need to "resist the devil," for he shall be "chained :" no call for hard-won victories over the world, — for "the world, and the lust thereof," shall have "passed away."

" There remaineth a rest (Heb. iv. 9).

But now,

"It is high time to awake out of sleep" (Ro. xiii. 11).

Now, "do thy diligence in every way."

"Take heed unto thyself, and to the doctrine" (1. Ti. iv. 16).

"O Jerusalem, that bringest good tidings, lift up thy voice with strength : lift it up, be not afraid" (Is. xli. 9).

" Reprove, rebuke, exhort" (2 Ti. iv. 2).

"Make straight in the desert an highway for our God" (Is. xl. 3).

And first of all, and for the sake of all,

" That good thing which was committed unto thee, keep" (2 Ti. i. 14).

" Hold fast that which thou hast, that no man take thy crown" (Rev. iii. 11).

"The people that know their God shall be strong, and do exploits" (Dan. xi. 32).

ARE ALL APOSTLES?

LOOKING at the immensity of the work, realizing in some faint way the glory of it, one often wishes heartily that one could do more : which is a very wise and right desire, and well open to fulfilment. But what is neither wise, right, nor practical, is to wish to do everything you see others do, and exactly as they do it. They have their work, you have yours : and if you try to measure the respective size and importance of the two, you will probably blunder straight along, and get thoroughly discouraged.

The Bible lays great stress upon "edifying" — building up. "Edify one another," edify the church, — but nobody ever yet saw a building on which everyone did precisely the same sort of work. It is all to the same true end : and so, steadily, surely, the wall rises, the windows look out, the beams fit in. And when things are right — in one small church, or the great Church univer- sal — the work goes on after this grand old pattern.

"They helped every one his neighbour; and every one said to his brother, Be of good courage. So the carpenter encouraged the goldsmith, and he that smootheth with the hammer him that smote the anvil, saying, It is ready for the sodering; and he fas- tened it with nails, that it should not be moved " (Is. xli. 6, 7).

It is a heathen example, but very ad- mirable. Each one found he had plenty to do, and yet could admire and cheer on the work of the rest : each saw the great importance of other men's doing what he could not. The very New Testament idea, also, you see.

"For the body is not one member, but many."

"And the eye cannot say unto the hand, I have no need of thee : nor again the head to the feet, I have no need of you" (1 Co. xii. 14, 21).

I suppose that mistake is sometimes made. But there is another, I fancy, much more common among us. For we who are only hands and feet, do often disparage our work ; looking up to the wise head, the bright eye, and feeling our own place in life to be dull and insignificant. Yet it is not so.

"If the whole body were an eye, where were the hearing ?" (1 Co. xii. 17).

Your idea would barter away the full-grown, well-developed figure of a man, for

the conventional cherub — all head and
wings.

Change the image, and you will see this
more clearly. Every single stone in the wall,
— dim it may be, and inconspicuous, but
fitted to its place and filling it well, — is as
truly important to the great edifice, as the
carved coping at which all men look. Set
you up on a high enough pole, you think,
and you could be an electric light with anybody : and maybe you could. And yet :

" Those members of the body which seem
to be more feeble, are necessary (1 Co.
xii. 22).

I am beginning to have a tender liking
for the despised old lamps, now banished
to the humblest highways, and doing their
brightest at the muddiest corners. Enough
of them would light the city, with a more
human glow, and no deadly wires in connection.

" Oppositions of science, falsely so called " (1 Ti. vi. 20).

" Thou hast corrupted thy wisdom by reason of thy brightness " (Ez. xxviii. 17).

So the words come to me : Our mental Broadway is rather a lurid place just now.

Never be dissatisfied with what you have to do.

" Now hath God set the members every one of them in the body, as it hath pleased him " (1 Co. xii. 18).

Your place in life, your work, your circumstances (unless your own wilful misdoing has spoiled them all) are just the Lord's wise, loving plan, marked out for *you*. When you complain of them, your complaint is against him. I think restlessness would well nigh die out of the world, if men but laid this to heart.

But you would like to do something that counts, — everything counts. Men are

saved — as stones are laid — one by one.
You may at least come out like that delightful little boy who having but one cent to
put in the plate, was desperately afraid it
was too small to be counted. Imagine then
his joy, when the minister read out:

"Our collection to-day amounts to fifty
dollars — and one cent!"

It will be something, to have swelled the
countless multitude by even one: to hear —

"Inasmuch as ye did it unto one of the
least of these —"

If a pulpit is denied you, cannot you
preach in the street? if you may not reform
a neighbourhood, can you not teach at home?
Not arithmetic, or even Latin and Greek,
but "the weightier matters of the law: judgment, mercy, and faith." "Ye are the salt
of the earth," — do all who come near you
feel the wholesome, purifying stimulation?
"Ye are the light of the world," — do your

own households see their way the clearer for that glad shining? One might take up the thought of "Your Mission," and carry it on almost indefinitely, setting the so-called little over against the so-called great.

> If you cannot be a leader
> In the crowd that pours along;
> Raise the fallen, lying prostrate
> Under foot amid the throng.
> If you cannot fire the nation, —
> If you cannot stir the race, —
> Lay cool hands on aching foreheads,
> Give sad hearts a resting-place.
> If you cannot reach the strangers,
> Gather in the men you know;
> Teach your friend the way to glory, —
> Draw your comrades where you go.
> Though your work be never mentioned,
> Though your name may not appear,
> Speak one word for "Jesus only,"
> And the Lord at least will hear.

It is one of the prettiest things in the world, to see how the broken walls of Jeru-

salem were built up in the days of Nehemiah.
And note first the absence of all hurry, not-
withstanding the need of haste. The wall
of Jerusalem was down, her gates burned
with fire, and impassable heaps of rubbish
lay on every hand. The case was urgent
enough. Yet before he even began to talk
about it, Nehemiah went alone at night, and
studied the whole thing out for himself: as
a young minister might word by word go
over the text :

"The whole world lieth in wickedness"
(1 Jn. v. 19).

Then, gathering the great work into his
arms, as it were ; knowing also to what full-
est extent he was ready to pledge himself :
the whole-hearted Israelite could say with
strongest persuasion :

"Come, and let us build up the walls of
Jerusalem" (Neh. ii. 17).

Telling then the wonderful providences

of God thus far, until the slow hearts of the people kindled.

"And they said, Let us rise up and build. So they strengthened their hands for this good work" (Neh. ii. 18).

Of course at once broke out a storm of laughter and scorn, upon the "remnant" that planned such great things. Convert the world with a handful of missionaries? turn men from their wicked courses by *your* weak efforts?

"What do these feeble Jews? will they fortify themselves? will they sacrifice? will they make an end in a day? will they revive the stones out of the heaps of the rubbish which are burned?

"Even that which they build, if a fox go up, he shall even break down their stone wall" (Neh. iv. 2, 3).

Like the questions in our own day: Can you ever reclaim a drunkard? Will your

heathen converts stand? And the despised ones gave back the only answer
that is worth a straw.

"The God of heaven, he will prosper us;
therefore we his servants will arise and
build" (Neh. ii. 20).

Then how they laboured, in the strength
of such faith and purpose! It was ideal
church work; for it was,

"As every man hath received the gift"
(1 Peter iv. 10).

"Every man according to his several
ability" (Matt. xxv. 15).

You can see differences: all had not
means alike,—still more, all did not labour alike with what they had; and there
was different work to do. The high priest
began it: he and his brethren the priests
taking first what seemed to them the most
important; even that "sheep gate" through
which the sacrifices were brought. They

builded and finished it, even to the last bit
of cleansing and consecration. And it is
pretty to see, that while they wrought thus
as it were for the whole congregation, some
of the congregation quietly wrought for
them. Eliashib the high priest builded
the sheep gate; and meanwhile Meremoth
the son of Urijah repaired "from the door
of the house of Eliashib even to the end
of the house of Eliashib;" evidently thinking that after his specially public labours,
the high priest ought to rest.

A stretch of solid building, from the
foundations up, followed the "sheep gate;"
finished bit by bit by one and another in
turn, even as far as "the fish gate;" which
also in its measure was well and thoroughly
done, until beams and doors and locks and
bars were all in place. Some might say,
what use in *finishing* any part, while so
much was not even begun? What need of

bolts and bars on the gate, with a breach in the wall ten feet away? But these builders were out-and-out men, and would have their work self-supporting before they left it.

And now came a bit of repair, — and another, — and another: rubbish to clear away, and if anything good was left, to adapt it and build it in. Repairing seems like comparatively easy work, and yet perhaps it needs just as deep devotion and whole-souled purpose. For when it came the turn of the Tekoites to repair,

"Their nobles put not their necks to the work of their Lord" (Neh. iii. 5).

And you cannot do much with the tips of your fingers. "The wise woman of Tekoah" seems to have had some foolish compatriots. Nehemiah records it, but we do not read that anybody stopped to comment: they were all too eagerly busy. It is refreshing to turn to those heartier souls, and catch even at this far-off distance the clink of their tools. New gates rose up, old gates were put to rights; and "fortification" strengthened the more exposed places of the built-up wall. Every now and then, too, there is a noteworthy bit of sideway description. One man repairs " *over against his house* " — a place neglected by some builders. Then we have a shew of women's hands amid the universal masculinity.

" Next to him repaired Shallum, . . . he and his daughters " (Neh. iii. 12).

They were able to help him — he was willing they should. Then Baruch " earnestly repaired another piece." It may not have been a large piece, but we know it was good work.

" With good will doing service, as to the Lord, and not to men " (Eph. vi. 7).

And one — was he an invalid? was he a poorest man? — accomplished but this: he " repaired over against his chamber."

"She hath done what she could" (Mark xiv. 8).

Yet even this, you see, would by and by reach round the world.

So the work went on. Sometimes a rich man repaired a great piece; or a knot of friends and neighbours took hold together: "the ruler of part of Mizpah," "the men of Jericho." But next to them would be "Uzziah of the goldsmiths," or "Hananiah the son of one of the apothecaries:" or unknown "Benjamin and Hashub," repairing together "over against their house." I perceive also that "the Tekoites repaired another piece," — so perhaps they got stirred out of their lukewarmness, and did better service.

"So built we the wall; and all the wall was joined together unto the half thereof: for the people had a mind to work" (Neh. iv. 10).

You see the grand result, and the simple explanation. But of course things could not long run on so smoothly.

"They that will live godly in Christ Jesus shall suffer persecution:" and these old builders found it true.

Then as now the walls of Jerusalem must rise under fire; and this record is well worth studying out. It is such an every-day, human story, that might have been written for our own time. How the world laughed and then threatened; how Judah lost heart and declared themselves tired; how Jews dwelling among the world, came with big eyes and bigger stories of what the world would do. How Nehemiah —loyal heart!—never faltered, but keeping the people well to their work (great virtue in that) gave the one watchword: Remember the Lord.

"Be not ye afraid of them: remember

the Lord, which is great and terrible"
(Neh. iv. 14).

Adding then the tenderest plea :

"And fight for your brethren, your sons,
and your daughters, your wives, and your
houses."

Remember — and fight : the far-off origi-
nal, you see, of " Pray — and keep your
powder dry."

Do you think the injunction is out of
date ? the plea grown old ? Does this gay
nineteenth century need newer doctrine ?
Alas, look at the ruined lives, the great
houses left desolate, the floods of sorrow
and evil which rolling up to the broken
walls of Jerusalem, and finding them un-
watched, flows in upon the city.

They set a worthy pattern in Nehemiah's
day. After that first brush with discour-
agement, they returned all of them to the
wall, "every man to his work."

" They which builded on the wall, and they that bare burdens, with those that laded, every one with one of his hands wrought in the work, and with the other held a weapon. For the builders every one had his sword girded by his side, and so builded " (Neh. iv. 17, 18).

That was the position, even for those who were too weak or too young to be more than armour bearers.

" So we laboured in the work, and half of them held the spears from the rising of the morning till the stars appeared " (Neh. iv. 20).

And it has its deep meaning, even for us.

" Thou therefore endure hardness, as a good soldier of Jesus Christ " (2 Ti. ii. 3).

" Fight the good fight " (1 Ti. vi. 12).

" Earnestly contend for the faith once delivered to the saints " (Jude 3).

And also Nehemiah's trumpet has its counterpart in modern times : what though the peculiar metal which gave his its ring, is getting to be rare and very precious.

"The work is great and large, — he reminded them, — and we are separated upon the wall, one far from another. In what place therefore ye hear the sound of the trumpet, resort ye thither unto us : our God shall fight for us " (Neh. iv. 19, 20).

Do you recognize that call when you hear it? For even in this day of uncertain sounds, the rallying trumpet may still be heard. When a Christian minister calls for workers ; when a missionary asks for reinforcements ; when heathen beg for teachers, and Bible women say, Must we give up this district for want of funds? — then, as at Sinai, "the trumpet soundeth long;" and with a tone only second in solemnity to that. It may be where fresh

forces attack the Sabbath gate ; or storm
up against the builders at the breach that
drink has made : a flight of Sanballat's
arrows (" What do these feeble Jews ? ") may
fall in one place ; the faint-heartedness of
Judah (" We are not able to build,") may
thin the ranks in another. But wherever
it is whence the trumpet sounds, to those
hard-pressed ones, whoever they may be,
" resort ye " all. " Our God shall fight for
us ;" you are not helping a doubtful cause.
Do you think I forget my own words, and
now *enjoin* you to be " in twenty places at
once " ? Yes, but not in the way I depre-
cated then. We all know what it is to send
our hearts to the front ; and unable to go
ourselves, to turn out every scrap of aid,
comfort, and power the house affords, and
then speed it on : so really fighting all along
the line. Time will be given in one place,
money in another : words, thoughts, prayers,

influence, will all "strive mightily" with
every hard-pressed band of workers. You
can shew countenance at least ; and many
a surrounded Board of Managers would be
glad of even that. Do you remember the
answer of the young soldier, when they
asked him rather scornfully what *he* could
do ? Said he : "I can stop a bullet that
might kill a better man !"

One more objection comes up. "Our
God shall fight for us," said Nehemiah : if
so, why call on *us ?* But you may notice
that the wise old Jew makes the only legitimate use of the promise, with it urging
men to do their utmost.

"The Lord is with you, while ye be with
him" (2 Chr. xv. 2).

So God has arranged it, and it is useless
to ask why. Stress almost unbounded is
laid upon human agency ; and if every one
else had answered some special summons,

the call would still be for you to do what you could. Israel had triumphed, "God had subdued the king of Canaan" before their forces; "the Lord discomfited Sisera," and delivered him into Barak's hand: it was all done, and all the Lord's doing. But two weighty sentences point the great song of thanksgiving.

"Praise ye the Lord for the avenging of Israel, when the people willingly offered themselves" (Jud. v. 2).

And then the stern naming of those who "came not to the help of the Lord, to the help of the Lord against the mighty."

UNTIL THE EVENING.

DOES it appall you?—
"This sore travail that God hath given to the sons of men to be exercised therewith" (Eccle. i. 13).

So Solomon felt.

"I looked on all the works that my hands had wrought, and on the labour that I had laboured to do; and, behold, all was vanity and vexation of spirit, and there was no profit under the sun" (Eccle. ii. 11).

Solomon even went further, and "hated life:" as many a lesser man has done since then. And, as I said, the work of the world has not ceased, but rather grown greater; and the turmoil is doubled, and

demands are heaped up ; and "there is no
discharge." "Man goeth forth unto his
work and to his labour until the evening,"
—and will, until the everlasting day shall
dawn. And yet how grand, how wholesome, how delicious, is work: for us, the
Lord's children, this part of the curse has
become a blessing, the thorns and the thistles bear blooms and fruit. How then, do
we not get tired, "like other men"? do we
not feel the thorn-pricks too?

"I am not able to bear all this people
alone," —said Moses (Num. xi. 15).

"I, even I only, am left," —said Elijah,
—"and they seek my life to take it away"
(1 Kings xix. 10).

Jonah fainted, and "wished in himself to
die" (Jonah iv. 8), under the buffeting of
an east wind of unusual power.

Even Paul was "pressed above measure,"
—poor tired servants, getting dazed in the

mêlée. But I think none of them ever
"hated labour;" and a word, a question,
from their Master set them all to rights.
Just a touch of his hand, as it were, letting
them know they were not alone. *They*
wish to "stand idle," in a world where
they could be "workers together with
Him"? "Spend and be spent" was their
motto; neither was life itself counted dear
in comparison. Fainting and frightened
and weary they might be, now and then,
but never seeking their discharge; never
calling life, as the unhired people do, "one
long disappointment."

What then did Solomon mean? he was
the wisest of men, and ought to know.
And he *did* know: he tasted to the full the
"vanity and vexation of spirit" in things
done merely for oneself.

"Yea, I hated all my labour which I had
taken under the sun: because I should

leave it unto the man that shall be after me. And who knoweth whether he shall be a wise man or a fool? yet shall he have rule over all my labour wherein I have laboured, and wherein I have shewed myself wise under the sun. This also is vanity" (Eccle. ii. 18, 19).

"Vanity" enough!

"He heapeth up riches, not knowing who shall gather them" (Ps. xxxvii. 9).

He plans the pulling down his barns and the building greater, and "that very night," perhaps, his soul is required of him.

"Then whose shall those things be?" (Lu. xii. 20).

"So is he that layeth up treasure for himself, and is not rich toward God" (Lu. xii. 21).

"Therefore I went about to cause my heart to despair of all the labour which I took under the sun.

"For what hath man of all his labour, and of the vexation of his heart, wherein he hath laboured under the sun? For all his days are sorrows, and his travail grief; yea, his heart taketh not rest in the night" (Eccle. ii. 20, 22, 23).

It is a weary outlook, over an alkaline plain. For it was all done for "*me.*" "I builded me houses," "I made me gardens," "I gathered me silver and gold;" doing it too with complete success. And it has a pleasant sound.

"Whatsoever mine eyes desired I kept not from them, I withheld not my heart from any joy" (Eccle. ii. 10).

"The kingdoms of this world, and the glory of them," do look attractive from certain points of view; and perhaps no one ever swept on his earthly course more triumphantly than Solomon.

"King Solomon passed all the kings of

the earth in riches and wisdom" (2 Chr. ix. 22).

"My heart rejoiced in all my labour," he says, exulting in success. But then set in the inevitable recoil. Who should possess it all, when Solomon's hands let go? what should become of the royal rooms, the heaped up treasure? Who should complete these works, who keep up those? Whose should be the "four thousand stalls, with their horses;" the "weight of gold;" the "traffic of the spice merchants;" the ships that every three years came bringing "gold and silver, ivory, apes, and peacocks"? If only there had been a freight or express train to the other world!—But no: the stern law: "When he dieth he shall carry nothing away: his glory shall not descend after him" (Ps. xlix. 17), was as unbending for the king as for the poorest beggar in his streets, who indeed had nothing to carry. And again the poor rich king who "withheld not his heart from any good" save one, cried out :

"Vanity of vanities : all is vanity."

"Whosoever drinketh of this water shall thirst again" (Jn. iv. 13).

And taking Solomon's stand-point, we might well join him in praising "the dead more than the living." But now just turn things round, and begin with, "Seek first the kingdom." For those whose life is "hid with Christ," who do all things in his name, seeking his glory not their own ; for them the world is a wide harvest field, and the mere work is glory. When "life is to do the will of God," no disappointment is possible ; neither can failure come in.

> "I run no risks, for come what will,
> Thou always hast Thy way."

" Of the increase of his government and peace, there shall be no end " (Is. ix. 7).

Therefore working for that, you cannot fail. " Sovereigns die, and sovereignties," — said Carlyle : " how all dies, and is for a time only, yet fancies itself real ! " But this of which we speak, is

" The everlasting kingdom of our Lord and Saviour Jesus Christ " (2 Pe. i. 11).

" Whose dominion is an everlasting dominion, and his kingdom is from generation to generation " (Dan. iv. 34).

It is a bank that cannot break : and cent per cent but faintly shadows forth the "good measure, pressed down, and shaken together, and running over," — of the dividends. Take all the stock in it you can. And do not blame me for using an everyday figure : one sometimes sees great things best so.

Thus living, not only for but with the

Lord ; going hour by hour and day by day close after his leading ; we get rid, too, of the pain of unfinished work. Up to this moment " it is done as thou hast commanded ; " and a sudden call to the Presence Chamber means only that further work here was not ours to do.

" Other men laboured, and ye have entered into their labours " (Jn. iv. 38).

So yet other men into ours. You think nobody can carry on your work so well as you yourself ? But if it is the Lord's work, probably he knows about that : if not, indeed, it matters little what is done with it; it is sure to be burned up, sooner or later.

Doubtless there were other churches and Christians for Paul to visit and strengthen, — yet he could say :

" I have finished my course " (2 Ti. iv. 7).

And assuredly he had thought of many further things he might do, — but still :

" I am now ready to be offered up " (2 Ti. iv. 6).

And when a man says " now " in that connection, he means it. The Lord knew best, in this as in other things.

" Thy counsels of old are faithfulness and truth " (Is. xxv. 1).

Could anything be better? And the Lord's faithful soldiers are not " retired upon half pay," but only ordered to report for higher duty ; called to join their regiments in the better land.

> " One army of the living God,
> To his command we bow :
> Part of his host have crossed the flood,
> And part are crossing now."

This is the grand, simple, every-day truth for us all, — and yet I believe many a one gets little good from it. All very well for

Paul, you think, but for you —*your* work never seems to amount to much. The labour is hard, the results discouraging.

"It is a glorious thing," said one of our soldiers on the battle-field, " to die looking up." — But it is also a glorious thing to *live* looking up. Remember,

"We are labourers together with God" (1 Co. iii. 9).

"Fellow helpers to the truth" (3 Jn. 8).

"Your work of faith, and labour of love, and patience of hope in our Lord Jesus Christ" (1 Th. i. 3), can never be in vain.

"I hated life," — said poor King Solomon, —"because the work that is wrought under the sun is grievous unto me.

"I looked on all the works that my hands had wrought, and on the labour that I had laboured to do: and, behold, all was vanity and vexation of spirit, and there was no profit under the sun" (Eccle. ii. 11).

True again, O wise-foolish king, of things done only for oneself.

" What shall it profit a man, if he shall gain the whole world, and lose himself, or be cast away ? " (Mark viii. 36).

But of lives lived humbly " in the name of the Lord Jesus," a greater than Solomon has answered :

" Write : Blessed are the dead that die in the Lord from henceforth : Yea, saith the Spirit, that they may rest from their labours ; and their works do follow them " (Rev. xiv. 13).

" Mine elect shall long enjoy the work of their hands " (Is. lxv. 22).

Yes, for you, O faithful servants, the crooked things *shall* " be made straight," and " that which is wanting " *shall* be numbered : even " the years eaten by the caterpillar and the locust shall be restored."

" He that goeth forth and weepeth, bearing precious seed, shall doubtless come again with rejoicing, bringing his sheaves with him " (Ps. cxxvi. 6).

" The world passeth away, and the lust thereof : but he that doeth the will of God, abideth for ever " (1 Jn. ii. 17).

Wherefore, " Let the peace of God rule in your hearts, to the which also ye are called in one body ; and be ye thankful " (Col. iii. 15).

University Press : John Wilson & Son, Cambridge.